Published by
PEACHTREE PUBLISHING COMPANY INC.
1700 Chattahoochee Avenue
Atlanta, Georgia 30318-2112
www.peachtree-online.com

Text © 2021 by Michelle Robinson
Illustrations © 2021 by Jez Tuya

First published in Great Britain in 2021 by Anderson Press Ltd.,
20 Vauxhall Bridge Road, London, SW1V 2SA.
First United States version published in 2021 by Peachtree Publishing Company Inc.
First trade paperback edition published in 2021 by Peachtree Publishing Company Inc.

The illustrations were digitally rendered using Adobe Photoshop and a Wacom Cintiq tablet.

Printed in January 2021 in China
10 9 8 7 6 5 4 3 2 1 (hardcover)
10 9 8 7 6 5 4 3 2 1 (trade paperback)
First Edition

HC ISBN: 978-1-68263-302-1
PB ISBN: 978-1-68263-365-6

Cataloging-in-Publication Data is available from the Library of Congress.

To David, Ellie and Finnemore —M. R.

To Mama and Papa —J. T.

RED TRUCK, YELLOW TRUCK

Michelle Robinson   Jez Tuya

PEACHTREE
ATLANTA

Red truck, yellow truck.

Red truck, yellow truck.

Tug truck. Tow truck.

Steady as you go, truck!

Empty truck...

load truck.

Straight back on the road, truck.

Stop, truck! Garbage truck. What a heap of muck, truck!

Squeeze, truck! Crush, truck! Never in a rush, truck.

Lift, truck. Shift, truck.

Shove away the drift, truck.

Honk, truck!

Blink, truck!

What's in there,
d'you think, truck?

Cow truck!

Can you spot the plow truck?

Wide truck. Tall truck!
Parked behind a wall truck.

Someone needs a clean truck.

Just where have you been, truck?!

Rolling,

dumping,

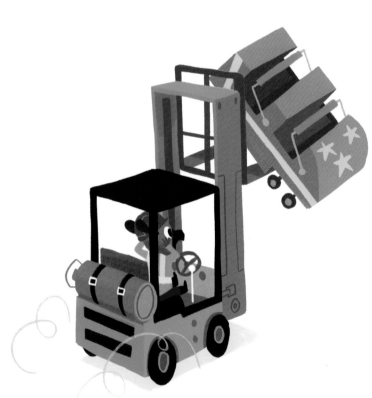

tipping, lifting!

Ladder raising!

Dirt pile shifting!

Climbing, squashing,

spilling, mixing!

Biffing, breaking...

...building, fixing!
The going gets tough—and the
trucks keep going!

Pushing and pulling and
heaving and towing.

Red truck, yellow truck...
which one would you drive?

Blue truck, green truck.

One,

two,

three,

four,

five!

On the road all day, truck!

On the road

all night!

All the way
back home, truck.

Engines off.

Beep tight!